James Orchard Halliwell-Philipps

## Memoranda

on Love's Labour's Lost, King John, Othello, and on Romeo and Juliet

James Orchard Halliwell-Philipps

**Memoranda**
*on Love's Labour's Lost, King John, Othello, and on Romeo and Juliet*

ISBN/EAN: 9783337092924

Printed in Europe, USA, Canada, Australia, Japan

Cover: Foto ©Andreas Hilbeck / pixelio.de

More available books at **www.hansebooks.com**

3

# MEMORANDA

ON

# Love's Labour's Lost, King John, Othello,

AND ON

# Romeo and Juliet.

BY

## HALLIWELL-PHILLIPPS, F.R.S.

LONDON:
PRINTED BY JAMES EVAN ADLARD.

1879.

# LOVE'S LABOUR'S LOST.

THE composition and structure of Love's
Labour's Lost unquestionably lead to a supposition that the main incidents were taken
from some old romantic story not yet discovered ; and that the tale, whenever it may be
found, will probably have been rightly conjectured to belong to the cycle of the lighter
romances of chivalry.  Douce is of opinion it
was borrowed from a French novel, but he
relies chiefly upon the names of the characters,
and on a palpable Gallicism in the fourth act;
while, on the other hand, the characters of the
Pedant and the Braggart, both so called in the
early copies, would induce us to believe that
the comedy was grounded upon an Italian
drama.  The story is partially founded on
history, as appears from the following passage
in the Chronicles of Monstrelet :—" Charles,
king of Navarre, came to Paris to wait on the
king.  He negociated so successfully with the
King and Privy Council, that he obtained a
gift of the castle of Nemours, with some of its

dependent castle-wicks, which territory was made a duchy. He instantly did homage for it, and at the same time surrendered to the king the castle of Cherburg, the county of Evreux, and all other lordships he possessed within the kingdom of France, renouncing all claims or profits in them to the king and to his successors, on condition that with the duchy of Nemours the king of France *engaged to pay him two hundred thousand gold crowns of the coin of the King our lord."* It will be seen from this passage, which was first pointed out by Mr. Hunter, that the link of connexion between history and the play is of a very slight kind ; but it is curious as showing us that the story used by Shakespeare was grounded in some degree on a real occurrence, although the main action of Love's Labour's Lost is of course fictitious. This king of Navarre died in 1425, and the time of the play may, therefore, be fixed shortly after that period.

It appears, from the title-page of the first edition of Love's Labour's Lost, that it was represented before Queen Elizabeth at Christmas, 1597; for although the year 1598 would not terminate, under the old method of computation, until March, 1599, there is every probability in favor of the drama having really been printed in 1598, the notices of Tofte and Meres proving that it was well known in that year. The same title-page further informs us that it was "newly corrected and augmented by W. Shakespere," a statement which induces the belief that the comedy had previously existed in a less perfect state than that in which it now appears. The internal evidence, indeed, clearly indicates its being a very early play, and it was probably, in its original form, one of the first dramas that Shakespeare composed. "The characters in this play," observes Coleridge, "are either impersonated out of Shakespeare's own multiformity by imaginative self-position, or out of such as a country town and a school-boy's observation might supply." The first position here suggested may of course be applied to any of the productions of the great master of dramatic art, but there appears, in Love's Labour's Lost, so many allusions to what was, in all probability, the literature of the poet's boyhood, and so much vernacular provincial phraseology, these indications, viewed in connexion with the general character of the play, lead to the conclusion above expressed.

The edition of 1598 is not mentioned in the registers of the Stationers' Company, the earliest notice of the play in those records appearing under the date of January, 1607, when it was transferred by Burby, with Romeo and Juliet and the Taming of a Shrew, to Linge :—" 22 Jan. 1606-7, Mr. Linge,—by direccion of a Court, and with consent of Mr. Burby, under his handwrytinge, these iij. copies, viz. Romeo and Juliett, Loues Labour Loste, 3. The Taminge of a Shrewe." On the nineteenth of November, in the same year, the comedy was transferred by Linge to John Smethwick,—"19 Nov. 1607,—John Smythick, under thandes of the wardens, these bookes folowing, whiche dyd belonge to Nicholas Lynge, 6. a booke called Hamlett, 9. the Taminge of a Shrewe, 10. Romeo and Julett, 11. Loues Labour Lost." If the play were printed by Linge, no copy of the impression has yet been discovered. The history of its copyright is, however, sufficiently clear from the above entries ; Burby, the original pro-prietor, parting with his interest in it in 1607 to Linge, who, in the same year, transfers it to Smethwick, one of the proprietors of the first folio. The last-named publisher, however, seems to have preserved an independent interest in the comedy, for it was published separately, under his auspices, in the year 1631. This edition was reprinted from the copy of the play in the first folio, and the latter was certainly reprinted from a playhouse copy of the first quarto edition of 1598, which, with that of 1623, are the only real authorities for the text of the comedy. On the title-page of the edition of 1631, it is stated to have been "acted by his Majesties Servants·at the Blackefriers and the Globe." It was also performed at Court early in the year 1605, the following entry occurring in the Revells Booke which relates to the period between October, 1604, and October, 1605,—"By his Majesties plaiers; Betwin Newers Day and Twelfe Day a play of Loves Labours Lost;" Cunningham's Revels' Accounts, p. 204.

Meres, in the Palladis Tamia, 1598, after mentioning the Two Gentlemen of Verona and the Comedy of Errors, speaks of, "his *Love labors lost*, his *Love labours wonne*," as two distinct pieces by Shakespeare, the latter being either the second name of a known play, or the title of one not now known to exist. It has been ingeniously conjectured that the title of Love Labours Wonne is merely another designation of the present comedy, and that Meres intended to write, "his Love Labors Lost *or* Love Labours Wonne;" a supposition probable so far as regards the fact of the object attained by the characters in the play itself, but wholly unsupported by any kind of evidence. "I can't well see," observes Gildon, in his Remarks, 1710, p. 308, "why the author gave this play this name." He was perhaps thinking of the estimate of Love, as he had expressed it in the Two Gentlemen of Verona, —"If haply *won*, perhaps a *hapless gain;*" and, on the other hand,—"If *lost*, why then a grievous *labour won.*" In real truth, Love's labour is not lost, for the gentlemen are all ensnared in his meshes, and they obtain the hands of the ladies on certain conditions, which are rather whimsical in their nature than impossible of performance.

The mode in which the title of the following comedy should be printed has been the subject of much discussion. In the title-page of the quarto edition of 1598, it is called, 'Loues labors lost,' but in the Palladis Tamia of Meres, published in the same year, it appears as, 'Loue labors lost,' and in Tofte's Alba, 1598,

Loves Labor Lost,' the latter form being also found in the Stationers' Registers for 1607. The running title of the first edition is, " A pleasant conceited Comedie called Loues Labor's lost," and, in the first folio of 1623, the title occurs twenty-three times, in each instance, 'Loues Labour's lost.' In the edition of 1631, it is ' Loues Labours lost ' on the title-page, the running title throughout the book being, ' Loues Labour's lost.' The second folio, in this respect, is copied from the first of 1623, but in the third folio of 1663, it appears in the form now usually adopted, viz., ' Love's Labour's Lost.' The balance of authority is so clearly in favor of this last title, the genitive case being rarely distinguished by apostrophes in the very early editions, that it is not advisable to alter it to the form given by Meres, who wrote from memory, and with no copy before him, or to the other title of, ' Love's Labour Lost ' (the last form also appearing, at a late date, in Langbaine, ed. 1691, p. 459). Mr. Knight has judiciously observed that the appearance of the apostrophe, in the edition of 1623, indicates the contraction of the verb, and shows that the author intended to call his play,

Love's Labour *is* Lost.' It is worthy of remark that the poem commencing " My flocks feed not," which has been attributed to Shakespeare, is entitled 'Loves labour lost,' in the edition of his poems which was published by Benson in 1640.

In the character of Holofernes, the poet no doubt intended a general satire upon the pedant of his day, a personage elsewhere delineated, in a similar style, by Sir Philip Sydney in the Lady of the May, where Rombus the school-master is another individual of the same type. The idea, however, has been entertained, by several eminent critics, that Shakespeare shadowed a real character under the name of Holofernes, and that the personage so satirized was John Florio, an Italian teacher in London contemporary with the great dramatist. The grounds for the formation of such an opinion are singularly inadequate to authorize the dogmatic manner in which it is promulgated by Warburton and supported by Farmer. Florio, it is assumed without the slightest evidence, had affronted Shakespeare by observing that " the plaies that they plaie in England are neither right comedies, nor right

tragedies ; but representations of histories
without any decorum." It is scarcely necessary to say that this remark may be general
in its application, without any peculiar reference to Shakespeare, who was not the only
writer of historical plays ; but even were it
admitted that Florio's words were directed
against his productions, there is nothing so
individually applicable in the character of
Holofernes to lead necessarily to the conclusion that it was delineated in the spirit of
retaliation. Florio and Shakespeare, more-
over, both acknowledged the same patron in
Lord Southampton, and they were more
probably friends than enemies. There could
not have existed any idea of rivalry between
two authors whose pursuits were so dissimilar,
and Shakespeare would hardly have endan-
gered his position with Lord Southampton
by holding up a favorite to ridicule, Florio,
in 1598, thus speaking of that nobleman,—
"in whose paie and patronage I have lived
some yeeres ; to whom I owe and vowe the
yeeres I have to live." This was in his
Worlde of Wordes, 1598, in the introduction
to which he is supposed to allude to Shakespeare, but without the slightest probability,

for the passage in which the presumed allusion occurs is in the midst of a long tirade against a person whose initials are H. S., and other circumstances are mentioned that do not well apply to the great dramatist. Richard Mulcaster, a schoolmaster and scholar of some eminence, also contemporary with Shakespeare, has likewise been conjectured, with as little likelihood, to have been the original prototype of the character of Holofernes. Malone is much more likely to be correct when he gives it as his opinion that "the character was formed out of two pedants in Rabelais : Master Tubal Holophernes, and Master Janotus de Bragmardo. Holophernes taught Gargantua his A. B. C. ; and afterwards spent forty-six years in his education. We have, however, no specimen in Rabelais of his method of teaching, or of his language ; but the oration of Janotus de Bragmardo for the recovery of the bells, is exactly what our poet has attributed to his pedant's leash of languages."

The exact date at which the comedy was written will perhaps never be ascertained. The question is rendered exceedingly intricate by the probability that it received additions from its author shortly before the year 1598. Little or no reliance can be placed on the mention of the dancing-horse, the allusion to that animal in Tarlton's Jests being no satisfactory evidence that it was exhibited before the death of that clown, and the notice in the early manuscript of Donne's Satires, transcribed in 1593, proving that it was known at the latter period. The allusion to Ajax is probably more important, as it appears to show that the comedy, in its present form, was written between 1596, the era of the publication of Sir John Harington's celebrated work, and 1598. The year 1597, as the date of the composition of the amended drama, agrees very well with all the external and internal evidences at present accessible.

A similarity has been pointed out by Chalmers between what Dr. Johnson calls the "finished representation of colloquial excellence" at the commencement of the fifth act, and a passage in Sydney's Arcadia, where he says, speaking of Parthenia, "that which made her fairnesse much the fairer was that it was but a faire embassador of a most faire mind, full of wit, and a wit which delighted more to judge itselfe then to show itselfe: her speech being as rare as precious; her silence without sullennesse; her modestie without affectation; her shamefastnesse without ignorance: in summe, one that to praise well, one must first set downe with himselfe what it is to be excellent; for so she is." Sydney's Arcadia was first published in 1590, but the similarity here pointed out is scarcely forcible enough to prove that there was any plagiarism. The coincidence was very likely quite accidental. Another allusion, that which is supposed to refer to the first and second "causes," and other terms, as promulgated in Saviolo's treatise on Quarrels, 1595, is of equal uncertainty. It is very possible that the technical words used by Shakespeare are also to be found in more than one other work.

In an obscure and exceedingly rare poem by Robert Tofte, entitled, Alba, the Months Minde of a Melancholy Lover, 8vo. Lond. 1598, there is an interesting and curious notice of an early performance of this comedy, which the author appears to have seen on the stage some time before the publication of his poem. It is also deserving of notice as one of the earliest extrinsic accounts of any of Shakespeare's undisputed dramas. Tofte's lines, viewed in

connexion with the other early notices of the
comedy, serve to show that Love's Labour's
Lost was a popular play during the life-time
of the author, when perhaps its satire was best
appreciated. Towards the close of the following century, it had so completely fallen in
general estimation, that Collier, who, although
an opponent of the drama, was not an indis-
criminate censurer of Shakespeare, says that
here the "poet plays the fool egregiously, for
the whole play is a very silly one;" Short View
of the Immorality and Profaneness of the
English Stage, 1699, p. 125. In 1762, the
author of a tasteless alteration of this play
hints that what remains of Shakespeare in the
new comedy will be amply sufficient "to please
the town." A complete appreciation of Love's
Labour's Lost was reserved for the present
century, several modern psychological critics of
eminence having successfully vindicated its title
to a position amongst the best productions of
the great dramatist. Amongst these, Coleridge,
with an enthusiasm aroused by the numerous
marks of genius exhibited in this comedy, has
penned a glowing criticism which should ever
find a place in future editions :—"If this juve-
nile drama had been the only one extant of our

Shakespeare, and we possessed the tradition only of his riper works, or accounts of them in writers who had not even mentioned this play, how many of Shakespeare's characteristic features might we not still have discovered in Love's Labour's Lost, though as in a portrait taken of him in his boyhood! I can never sufficiently admire the wonderful activity of thought throughout the whole of the first scene of the play, rendered natural, as it is, by the choice of the characters, and the whimsical determination on which the drama is founded —a whimsical determination certainly, yet not altogether so very improbable to those who are conversant in the history of the middle ages, with their Courts of Love, and all that lighter drapery of chivalry, which engaged even mighty kings with a sort of serio-comic interest, and may well be supposed to have occupied more completely the smaller princes, at a time when the noble's or prince's court contained the only theatre of the domain or principality."

Love's Labour's Lost is not a favorite play with the general reader, but the cause of its modern unpopularity is to be sought for in the circumstance of its satire having been principally directed to fashions of language that have long passed away, and consequently little understood, rather than in any great deficiency of invention. When it has been deeply studied, there are few comedies that will afford more gratification. It abounds with touches of the highest humour; and the playful tricks and discoveries are conducted with so much dexterity, that, when we arrive at the conclusion, the chief wonder is how the interest could have been preserved in the development of so extremely meagre a plot. Rightly considered, this drama, being a satire on the humour of conversation, could not have been woven from a story involving much situation other than the merely amusing, or from any plot which invited the admission of the language of passion; for the free use of the latter would have been evidently inconsistent with the unity of the author's satirical design.

# THE DANCING HORSE.

THE "dancing horse" was a celebrated animal, exhibited by a Scotchman named Banks, which was often alluded to under that title by contemporary writers. This horse, which was a bay in colour, was taught tricks and qualities of a nature then considered so wonderful, that the exhibitor was popularly invested with the powers of magic, and both of them obtained an European celebrity; yet so difficult is it to recover information respecting characters and exhibitions of this description, the reader will scarcely be enabled to gather a connected history from the following curious notices, although they are of great value in estimating the degree of credit to be attached to the arguments which have been adduced on behalf of assigning a date to the composition of the play from the allusion in the text. Much of this difficulty arises from the uncertain degree of credit to be assigned to the earliest writers who mention the horse, and we are met, on the threshold of enquiry, by a doubt respecting the exact truth of a singular anecdote, which, were it to be depended upon, would not only prove that Banks was originally a retainer in the service of the Earl of Essex, but that he had exhibited his horse some time before the date of Tarlton's death, which took place in September, 1588. The anecdote alluded to is found in 'Tarlton's Jests,' a compilation first published about the year 1600, and it is sufficiently curious to be given entire. In 1601, the horse is described as being *about* twelve years old, and if this statement be accepted as a little below the real fact of the case, it is not impossible that the animal was exhibited for the first time shortly before the decease of Tarlton. There is a notice of it in the Epigrams of Davies, hereafter quoted, generally stated to have been printed in 1596, in which Banks is said to have spoken the praises of the horse "long-a-gon." On the other hand, it is called a "yong nagg" in the latter part of the year 1595.

*Tarlton's greeting with Banks his horse.*—There was one Banks, in the time of Tarlton, who served the Earle of Essex, and had a horse of strange qualities, and being at the Crosse-Keyes in Gracious-streete, getting mony with him, as he was mightily resorted to, Tarlton then, with his fellowes, playing at the Bell by, came into the Crosse-Keies, amongst many people, to see fashions; which Banks perceiving, to make the people laugh, saies, Signior, to his horse,—Go fetch me the veryest foole in the company. The jade comes immediately, and with his mouth drawes Tarlton forth. Tarlton, with merry words, said nothing but,—God a mercy, horse! In the end Tarlton, seeing the people laugh so, was angry inwardly, and said,—Sir, had I power of your horse, as you have, I would doe more then that. Whatere it be, said Bankes, to please him, I wil charge him to do it. Then, saies Tarlton, charge him to bring me the veriest whoremaster in this company. He shall, saies Banks. Signior, saies he, bring Master Tarlton here the veriest whore-master in the company. The horse leades his master to him. Then, God a mercy, horse! indeed, sayes Tarlton. The people had much ado to keepe peace; but Bankes and Tarlton had like to have squar'd, and the horse by to give aime. But ever after it was a by-word thorow London, "God a mercy, horse," and is to this day.—*Tarlton's Jests drawn into three Parts.*

The earliest indisputably authentic notice of Banks' horse yet discovered occurs in a copy of Donne's Satires in the British Museum, "Jhon Dunne his Satires, anno Domini 1593," preserved in MS. Harl. 5110, a MS. either written in that year, or an early copy probably from a transcript bearing that date :—

> But to a grave man he doth move no more,
> Then the wise politique horse would heretofore.

The horse seems to have attained a great degree of popularity as early as 1595, a ballad and tract on the subject having been published towards the close of that year, when the following entries occur in the books of the Stationers' Company:—" 1595, 14 Nov. Edward White,— Entred for his copie under thandes of both the wardens, a ballad shewing the strange qualities of a yong nagg called Morocco, vj.*d.*—17 December. Cutbert Burby,—Entred for his coppy under thandes of the wardens, Maroccus Extaticus, or Bankes bay horse in a traunce, vj.*d.*" The ballad appears to have perished, but a copy of the pamphlet has been preserved, and is thus entitled,—"Maroccus Extaticus, or Bankes Bay Horse in a Trance, a discourse set downe in a merry dialogue between Bankes and his beast, anatomizing some abuses and bad trickes of this age, written and intituled to mine host of the Belsavage, and all his honest guests, by John Dando, the wier-drawer of Hadley, and Harrie Runt, head ostler of Bosomes Inne ; Printed for Cuthbert Burby, 1595," 4to, with a woodcut on one of the leaves, in which the horse is represented standing on the hind legs with a stick in his mouth, and a pair of dice on the ground ready for the exhibition of the animal's sagacity. There is character in the representation of Banks, which may possibly be regarded as a rough portrait of him. The pamphlet itself is of very little importance in connexion with the history of Banks and his horse, but it is gathered from it that the latter was then being exhibited at the Bel-savage without Ludgate, an ancient London inn still remaining, which was a favorite place in Shakespeare's time, for such kinds of amusement. The following extract includes everything in the tract that is at all illustrative of the present subject :

"*Bankes.* And therewith mee thinkes I see him hang the hat upon the pin againe. Wast not so, Marocco ? I am glad, sir, to heare you so pleasant in the threshold of my discourse, for

I am come in purpose to debate a while and
dialogue with you, and therefore have at you
after your watering; laie out your lips and
sweep your manger cleane, and summon your
wits together, for I meane (by mine host leave),
to recreate my selfe awhile with your horsemanship.

"*Horse.* And I am as like, master, to shew
you some horse plaie as ere a nag in this
parish; for tis a jade can neither whihie nor
wag his taile, and you have brought me up
to both, I thanke you, and made me an under-
standing horse, and a horse of service, master,
and that you know.

"*Bankes.* I, Marocco, I know it, and
acknowledge it; and so must thou, if thou
have so much ingenuitie, confesse my kindnes,
thou art not onely but also bound to honest
Bankes, for teaching thee so many odde
prankes. I have brought thee up right
tenderly, as a baker's daughter would bring
up a cosset by hand, and allow it bread and
milke by the eie.

"*Horse. Majus peccatum habes;* master,
you have the more to answere, God helpe
you; for I warrant you (though I saie it that
should not saie it), I eat more provender in

foure and twentie houres, than two of the best geldings that Robin Snibor keeps, that a hires for two shillings a daie a peece."

The name of the horse was probably derived from that of the saddle, a particular kind of which, called the Morocco saddle, is described in Markham's Cavalarice, ed. 1617, vi. 52.

The grand exploit of this celebrated horse was the ascent of St. Paul's cathedral, which took place in the year 1600. The steeple of St. Paul's, in Decker's Dead Terme, 1608, is represented as saying,—" Some, seeing me so patient to endure crowes and dawes pecking at my ribs, have driven tame partridges over my bosome; others even riding over me, and capring upon my backe, as if they had bin curvetting on the horse, which in despight they brought to trample upon me." A marginal note explains these allusions as follows, —" Eight partridges on the top of Powles in an. 1597; a horse there likewise in an. 1600." This statement, published so shortly after the occurrence, is likely to be correct; and it is confirmed by a computation made in the Owles Almanacke, published in 1618, but in the following extract dating backwards from 1617, which refers the event to the same year,—

"Since the *dancing horse* stood on the top of Powles, whilst a number of asses stood braying below, seventeen yeares." The following are a few notices of this exploit, out of many more that might be collected :—

I, I, I ; excellent sumpter horses carry good cloaths : But, honest roague, come ; what news, what newes abroad ? I have heard a' the horses walking a' th top of Paules.—*Satiro-Mastix, or the Untrussing of the Humorous Poet,* 1602.

But afterward proved more beast then his horse, being so overwhelmed with whole cans, hoopes, and such drunken devices, that his English crowne weighed lighter by ten graines at his comming forth, then at his entering in ; and it was easier now for his horse to get up a top of Powles, then he to get up upon his horse ; the stirrup plaide mock holyday with him, and made a foole of his foote.—*The Meeting of Gallants at an Ordinarie, or the Walkes in Powles,* 1604.

May not the devil, I pray you, walk in Paul's, as well as the horse go a' top of Paul's, for I am sure I was not far from his keeper.— *The Blacke Booke,* 1604.

Could the little horse that ambled on the

top of Paul's carry all the people ? Else how could they ride on the roofs ?—*Northward Hoe*, 1607.

Yee have been either eare or eye witnesses, or both, to many madde voiages made of late yeares, both by sea and land, as the travell to Rome in certain daies, the wild morrise to Norrige, the fellowes going backward to Barwick, another hopping from Yorke to London, and the transforming of the top of Paules into a stable.—*Rowley's Search for Money*, 1609.

From hence (the top of Paul's steeple) you may descend, to talke about the horse that went up; and strive, if you can, to know his keeper; take the day of the moneth, and the number of the steppes, and suffer yourselfe to beleeve verily that it was not a horse, but something else in the likenesse of one.— *Decker's Guls Hornbook*, 1609.

The exploit is also made the subject of a somewhat amusing· anecdote in the Jests to make you Merie, 1607, a compilation attributed to Decker assisted by George Wilkins: —" When the horse stood on the top of Poules, a servingman came sweating to his maister, that was walking in the middle ile, and told him the wonder he had seene, and what multitudes of people were in the streetes staring to behold it ; the fellow most vehemently intreating his maister to goe and make one. Away, thou foole, sayd hee, what neede I goe so farre to see a horse on the top, when I can looke upon so many asses at the bottome ? O yes, sir, replyed the servingman, you may see asses heere every day, but peradventure you shall never see a horse there againe, though there were a thousand beasts in the cittie."

The year following the accomplishment of the ascent of St. Paul's, Banks crossed the Channel, and exhibited the horse at Paris, where its singular tricks excited the greatest astonishment, and led its owner into difficulties that were nearly proving of serious moment. The amazement with which the feats of Morocco were received in the French capital, has been graphically described by Jean de Montlyard, Sieur de Melleray, who was an eye-witness, in a long note to a French translation of the Golden Ass of Apuleius, 1602, which is certainly the most curious account of the dancing-horse that has yet been discovered, and fully deserves transcription, the rather as the few notices of it hitherto given have not

been made with great accuracy :—" Mais tout
cecy n'est rien au prix des estranges gesticula-
tions de cest incomparable cheval que nous
avons veu n'agueres à Paris, dressé par un
Ecossois à choses incroyables à ceux qui ne
les auront veuës. Le cheval est de moyenne
taile, bay, guilledin d'Angleterre, âgé d'environ
douze ans, son maistre l'appelle Moraco, et le
monstre à l'heure que nous escrivons cecy, l'an
1601, en la ruë S. Jacques au Lyon d'argent :
et depuis en d'autres quartièrs de la ville, au
grand estonnement de tous les spectateurs.
Il va querir tout ce qu'on luy jette en place et
l'apporte à guise d'un barbet. Il saulte et
gambade ainsi qu'un singe. Il se tient debout
à deux pieds, sur lesquels il marche tantost
avant, tantost arriere, puis à genoüil, ayant
neantmoins les pieds de derriere tous droits.
Son maistre jette un gand emmy la place, luy
commande d'aller querir, et le porter à celuy
de la compagnie´ qui porte (pour exemple) des
lunettes. Moraco le fait et, sans se tromper,
s'addresse à celuy qui les a devant les yeux.
Il luy commande de porter le mesme gand à
celuy ˙de la compagnie qui porte un manteau
doublé de telle ou telle estoffe ; ˙de pelluche
pour exemple : j'allegue ce que je luy ay veu

faire ; Moraco choisit entre plus de deux cens
personnes, celuy que son maistre luy designe
tout haut par quelque marque, et luy porte le
gand. Pour tesmoigner que Moraco cognoit
les couleurs, ou la dexterité de l'art de son
maistre, qu' aucun n'a sceu encore descouvrir,
s'il luy dit qu'il porte ce gand à une damoiselle
de la trouppe qui a (par rencontre) un manchon
de velours verd, ou d'autre couleur, il la va sans
se mesprendre trouver d'un bout de la sale à
l'autre. Nous l'avons veu faire cecy de deux
manchons à mesme heure, l'un verd, l'autre
violet, avec plusieurs autres traits trop longs
à reciter. Son maistre luy couvre les yeux
d'un manteau ; puis demande à trois de la
compagnie trois pieces differentes d'argent ou
d'or. Nous avons veu luy donner un sol, un
quart d'escu, un escu ; puis les mettre dans un
gand, desboucher son Moraco, luy demander
combien de pieces il y avoit dans le gand : le
cheval frapper trois coups de pied contre le
carreau pour dire trois. Plus son maistre
demander combien il y en avoit d'or : et
Moraco ne batre qu'un coup, pour dire une.
Item l'interroger combien de francs vaut
l'escu : et luy donner trois fois du pied en
terre. Mais chose plus estrange, parce que

l'escu d'or sol et de poids vaut encor main-
tenant au mois de Mars, 1601, plus que trois
francs, l'Escossois luy demanda combien de sols
valoit cest escu outre les trois francs, et Moraco
frappa quatre coups, pour denoter les quatre
sols que vaut l'escu de surcroist. L'Escossois
fait apporter un jeu de cartes, les mesle fort et
ferme, en fait tirer une par quelqu'un de l'as-
semblée : puis commande à son cheval de
heurter autant de coups que la carte vaut de
points : s'elle est rouge, qu'il frappe du pied
droit : si noire, du gauche. Ce que nous luy
avons veu faire d'un cinq de picque. Il luy
commande qu'il ait à marcher comme il feroit
s'il avoit à porter une damoiselle. Moraco fait
deux ou trois tours par la sale et va tres-
doucement l'amble. Qu'il marche comme s'il
portait un valet : il chemine un trot rude et
fascheux. Puis luy demande comme il feroit
si quelque escuyer estoit monté sur luy. Cet
animal se prend à faire des courbetes aussi
justes que aucun cheval en puisse faire, bons
et passades, et tous autres saults qu'on fait
faire aux chevaux de manege. Si son maistre
le tance comme faisant du lasche, et le menace
de le donner à quelque chartrier qui le fera
travailler tout son saoul, et luy baillera plus de

foüett que de foin : Moraco, comme s'il enten-
doit son langage, baisse la teste, et par d'autres
gestes faict cognoistre qu'il n'en est pas content :
il se laisse tomber en terre comme s'il estoit
malade ; roidit les jambes, demeure longue-
ment en ceste posture, et se contrefait si bien
qu'on le croiroit de fait estre mort.   Nous
avons veu son maistre le fouler aux pieds,
promettre neantmoins de luy pardonner si
quelqu'un de la compagnie demandoit pardon
pour luy.   Là dessus, pardonnez-luy (s'escria
quelqu'un des spectateurs du bout de la sale)
il fera bien son devoir.   Adonc l'Escossois luy
commanda qu'il se levast, et s'en allast remer-
cier celuy qui avoit requis et obtenu pardon
pour luy.   Moraco s'en alla choisir un homme
de poil roux, celuy voirement qui avoit servy
d'intercesseur : et pour signe de gratitude luy
mit la teste en son manteau, luy faisant beaucoup de caresses et demonstrations de recog-
noissance.   Apres cela, je vous mettray (ce luy
dit son maistre) a la poste pour vous desgourdir
les jambes, puisque vous ne voulez rien faire.
Moraco pour faire entendre qu'il est inutile à
tel service, leve une jambe en haut ; et feignant
y avoir mal, ne marche que de trois pieds.   Il
luy commande qu'il esternuë par trois fois.   Il

le fait sur le champ. Qu'il rie ; ille fait au cas pareil, montrant les dents et chanuissant des oreilles. Il donne un gand à quelqu'un de la trouppe, et commande à son Moraco de luy amener par le manteau l'homme auquel il l'a donné. Le cheval le va prende par le manteau, et l'estreint si fort avec les dents, que l'homme est constraint de la suivre : et se fait amener de mesme tous ceux qu'il veut, les luy designant par quelque marque, comme de pennache noir, blanc, rouge, &c. ; voire quelqu'un qui porte sous son aiselle un sac de papiers, encore qu'il le cache : ce que nous avons veu faire. Apres une infinité de tours de passe-passe, il luy fait danser les Canaries avec beaucoup d'art et de dexterité. Il marque avec une espingle un nombre de chiffre sur un gand ; puis envoye son Moraco cercher parmy la foule celuy qui tient le gand. Il le trouve incontinent. Et luy commandant de frapper en terre autant de fois que le chiffre vaut, il le fait tout ainsi que s'il avoit veu ledit chiffre et en eust entendu la valeur. Ce que nous luy avons veu faire d'un 8. Le magistrat estimant que cecy ne se peust faire sans magie, avoit quelque temps auparavant enprisonné le maistre, et sequestré le cheval : mais ayant depuis mani-

festement recogneu que ce n'est que par art et
par signes qu'il fait tout cela, il le fit eslargir,
et luy permit de faire montre de son cheval.
L'Escossois asseure n'y avoir cheval auquel il
n'en apprenne autant en un an."

The suspicion imbibed at Paris that the aid
of magic was invoked, alluded to at the close of
the above very curious account, was also entertained at other places. An adventure resulting
from this at Frankfort is thus described by
Bishop Morton, in his Direct Answer unto the
Scandalous Exceptions of Theophilus Higgons,
4to. Lond. 1609, p. 11,—"Which bringeth into
my remembrance a storie which Banks told me
at Franckeford from his own experience in
France among the Capuchins, by whom he was
brought into suspition of magicke because of
the strange feats which his horse Morocco
plaied (as I take it) at Orleance; where he, to
redeeme his credit, promised to manifest to the
world that his horse was nothing lesse then a
divell. To this end he commanded his horse
to seeke out one in the preasse of the people
who had a crucifixe on his hat; which done, he
bad him kneele downe unto it; and not this
onely, but also to rise up againe and to kisse it.
And now, gentlemen, quoth he, I thinke my

horse hath acquitted both me and himselfe; and so his adversaries rested satisfied : conceaving, as it might seeme, that the divell had no power to come neare the crosse." Markham, who is somewhat indignant that such suspicions should have been entertained, says, —"Now for those onely (speaking of the tricks which horses can be instructed to perform) which a horse will doe, as being unnaturall, strange and past reason, wee have had a full testimony in our time by the curtall which one Banks carryed up and downe and shewed both to princes and to the common people, which were so farre beyond conceit that it was a generall opinion, and even some of good wisdome have maintained the assertion, that it was not possible to bee done by a horse that which that curtall did but by the assistance of the devill; but, for mine owne part, I knowe that all which so thought were infinitely deceived, and these two reasons leade me thereunto, that first I perswade myselfe the man was exceeding honest, and secondly that I knowe by most assured tryals that there was no one tricke which that curtall did which I will not almost make any horse doe in lesse then a monthes practise." Sir K. Digby, in his

Nature of Bodies, ed. 1644, p. 321, says, "every one of us knoweth by what meanes his painefull tutor brought him to do all his trickes."

In 1609, Banks had the honor of receiving the patronage of Prince Henry. In the in-edited MS. Privy Purse expenses of his Royal Highness, preserved at the Rolls House, occur the following entries early in 1608-9 :—" 1 Januar : 1608 ; To Banks, for teaching of a litle naig to vaut, be his highnes comand, 2*li.* —2 February, 1608 ; To Mr. Banks, at his high : command, 6*li.*" Considering the value of money at that early period, these sums are of a liberal amount and testify to the extent of his reputation in all that related to the management of horses. The entries are also, perhaps, of some value in respect to the question of his social position, which seems to have been creditable. It appears from an early Lancashire pedigree quoted in Hunter's Illustrations, i. 265, that a "daughter of . . . . Banks, who kept the horse with the admirable tricks," married John Hyde of Urmston, the Hydes being an ancient county family of some importance. Banks is expressly noted by Markham in his Cavelarice as an "exceeding honest" man.

The particular allusion made by Shakespeare
to the horse refers to its power of counting
money, a feat for which it was early distinguished; Bishop Hall, in his Toothless Satyrs,
1597, speaking of "strange Morocco's dumbe
arithmeticke." Bastard, in his Crestoleros,
1598, informs us that it could "finde your
purse, and tell what coyne ye have." Jean
de Montlyard, as previously quoted, was in
utter astonishment at the wonderful manner
in which the horse calculated the value of
French money in 1601; and Sir K. Digby
observes that it "would tell the just number
of pence in any piece of silver coyne barely
shewed him by his master," Nature of Bodies,
ed. 1644, p. 321. The mode in which this
faculty was taught is set forth in Markham's
Cavelarice, 1607, in a very curious chapter
entitled,—" How a horse may be taught to
doe any tricke done by Bankes his curtall,"
and the portion of which, relating to this
quality, is worth quoting in connexion with
the calculating powers of Morocco alluded to
by the great dramatist :—" Now if you will
teach your horse to reckon any number by
lifting up and pawing with his feete, you shall
first with your rodde, by rapping him upon the

shin, make him take his foote from the ground,
and by adding to your rod one certaine word,
as *Up*, or such like, now when he will take up
his foote once, you shall cherrish him, and give
him bread, and when hee sets it uppon the
ground, the first time you shall ever say *one*,
then give him more bread, and after a little
pause, labour him againe at every motion,
giving him a bit of bread til he be so perfit
that, as you lift up your rod, so he will lift up
his foot, and as you move your rod downeward,
so he will move his foot to the ground ; and
you shall carfully observe to make him in any
wise to keep true time with your rod, and not
to move his foot when you leave to move your
rodde, which correcting him when he offends,
both with stroakes and hunger, he will soone
be carefull to observe. After you have brought
him to this perfectnesse, then you shall make
him encrease his numbers at your pleasure, as
from one to two, from two to three, and so
fourth, till in the end hee will not leave pawing
with his foote, so long as ever you move your
rod up and downe; and in this by long custome
you shall make him so perfect that, if you make
the motion of your rod never so little, or hard
to bee perceived, yet he will take notice of it ;

and in this lesson as in the other, you must also dyrect him by your eie, fixing your eyes upon the rod and uppon the horsses feete all the while that you move it; for it is a rule in the nature of horsses, that they have an especiall regard to the eye, face, and countenaunce of their keepers, so that once after you have brought him to know the helpe of your eye, you may presume he will hardly erre except your eye misguide him; and therefore ever before you make your horse doe any thing, you must first make him looke you in the face. Now after you have made him perfit in these observations, and that he knowes his severall rewardes, both for good and evill dooings, then you may adventure to bryng him into any company or assembly, and making any man think a number, and tell it you in your eare, you may byd the horse tell you what number the man did thinke, and at the end of your speech bee sure to saye last *Up:* for that is as it were a watch-worde to make him know what hee must doe, and whylest you are talking, you shall make him looke in your face, and so your eye dyrecting him unto your rodde, you may with the motions thereof make him with his foot declare the number before thought by the by-stander. From this you may create a world of other toyes, as how many maydes, howe many fooles, how many knaves, or how many rich men are amongst a multitude of gazing persons, making the worlde wonder at that which is neyther wonderfull nor scarce artificiall."

The feat alluded to above, and earlier in Bastard's Chrestoleros, 1598, of the horse singling out a knave, was probably accomplished by its master being enabled by signs to indicate to the animal any particular person. Something of this kind has been already noticed in the anecdote from Tarlton's Jests, and, according to Nash, 1596, the horse could distinguish a Spaniard from an Englishman. A more invidious quality was that of "discerning maids from maulkins," as it is stated in the romance of Don Zara del Fogo, 1660, which, although of course accomplished solely in accordance with the fancy of Banks himself, or perhaps left to the accidental choice of Morocco, must have been the cause of much merriment suited to the coarse manners of the age. The latter accomplishment is likewise hinted at in some curious lines in the Poet's Palfrey, a poem in Brathwait's Strappado for the Divell, 1615, from which it is also ascertained that two-pence was the usual price of admission to witness the exploits of the dancing-horse :—

If I'had liv'd but in our Banks his time,
I doe not doubt, so wittie is my jade,
So full of imitation, but in fine,
He would have prov'd a mirrour in his trade,
And told Duke Humphreis knights the houre to dine ;
Yea, by a secret instinct would had power,
To know an honest woman from a whoore. . . . .
Now, generous spirits that inhabit heere,
And love to see the wonders of this isle,
Compar'd with other nations, draw but neere,
And you shall see what was exprest ere-while ;
Your pay's but pence, and that's not halfe so deere,
If you remember, as was that same toy
Of Banks his horse, or Fenner's England's Joy.

The faculty of dancing, in which the horse appears to have attained great proficiency, and to have been the cause of its being invested with the title of the dancing-horse, was probably not the most extraordinary characteristic of Morocco, but it is frequently alluded to by contemporary writers. Jean de Montlyard asserts that he saw it dance the canaries very dexterously early in the year 1601. Previously, in Bastard's Chrestoleros, 1598, its power of dancing had been noticed, and several other allusions will be observed in extracts given in the present note, to which the following may be added :—

> Who, thus besotted, forthwith gins to bray,
> Attempteth eke like Bankes his horse to daunce.
> > *The Mastive, or a Young Whelpe of the Olde*
> > *Dogge,* n. d.

Never had the *dauncing horse* a better tread of the toe; never could · Beverley Faire give money to a more sound taborer, nor ever had Robin Hood a more deft Mayd Marian.—*Old Meg of Herefordshire,* 1609.

I will not be found at Sellengers-Round, although thou do call me a slouch. Banks's horse cannot prance a merrier dance, then rumbling and jumbling a clatter-de-pouch.—*A Pleasant Comedie entituled Hey for Honesty,* 1651.

To these may be added the following allusion to the horse making a curtesy, in the Cities New Poets Mock Show, 1659; a date which shows for how long a time the remembrance of this celebrated animal continued :—

> Now comes the mayor to the bar of course,
> To the judge he made legs like Banks's horse ;
> He could do no better; 'twas well 'twas no worse.

"This horse," observes Sir Kenelm Digby, "would restore a glove to the due owner, after his master had whispered that man's name in his eare." See also the extract from Jean de Montlyard, previously given. Markham, in his Cavelarice, after a few general preparative directions, says,—"then you may begin to teach him to fetch your glove, first by making him take your glove into his mouth and holding it, then by letting the glove fal to the ground and making him take it up, and lastly by throwing the glove a pretty way from you and making him fetch it and deliver it unto you; and every time he doth to your contentment you shal give him two or three bits of bread, and, when he offends you, then two or three strokes; or if you finde him verye wilful or unapt to conceive, then, as soone as you have corrected him, you shal put on his mussel, and let him stand for at least six hours after without meat, and then prove him again; yet you must, when your horse wil receive your glove, take uppe your glove, and fetch your glove, you shal then make him carrie a glove whither you wil, in this sort; first, you shall make him receive it in his mouth, and then pointing out a place with your rod, you shal

say unto him, *deliver*, and not leave repeating
that word, sometimes more sharpely, sometimes
gently, til he lay or at least bow his hed down
with it to that place where your rod pointed,
and then you shal cherrish him and give him
bread ; thus you shal labor and apply him
everie houre when he is hungry, till you have
made him that he wil carrie to anie place
against which you pointe your rod, and when
you saie, *deliver*, then to let it parte from his
mouth.   Then you shal cause two or three
by-standers to stande a prettie distaunce one
from another, and then giving the horsse the
glove, you shall with your rod point at him to
whome you woulde have him carrie it, and as
soone as hee comes neare, or but towardes the
party you point at, he shal put out his hande,
and receive the glove from him, and you shal
then cherrish the horsse, and give him breade,
and thus you shall do to every several by-
stander divers and sundry times, till the horse
bee so perfit that he will go to which or whom
you will point at ; and when he doth erre never
so little, you shall not faile first to bid him, *Be
wise*, and then if he amend not instantly, to
correct him ; this done, you shall make two
by-standers to stand close togethcr, and then

poynting at one of them, if the horse mistake
and looke more towards the other, you shall
byd him, *Be wise;* and then if he turne his
head towards the other, hee shall presently
receive the glove, and you shall cherrish the
horse."

There was yet another accomplishment
taught to Morocco, the value of which is
rather difficult to discover; but it is made
the subject of a curious discourse by Markham,
in which is described the method of compelling
a horse to perform certain functions at any
moment at the bidding of its master. There
is distinct evidence that this was one of the
attractions of the horse exhibited by Bankes, it
being hinted at by Bastard, in his Chrestoleros,
1598, and distinctly alluded to by Sir K. Digby,
in his treatise on the Nature of Bodies, ed.
1644, p. 321. See further in Markham's Cavelarice, 1607, a work on horsemanship, in which
an attribute to the popular fame of Banks is
found in the fact of a mention of his celebrated
horse being introduced even in the title-page,
where may be seen curious directions for teaching a horse this quality, though unfortunately
in language too coarse for republication.

The author of Humane Industry, or a History of most Manual Arts, 8vo. 1661, p. 173, observes,—"an asse hath not so dull a soul as some suppose, for Leo Afer saw one in Africa that could vie feats with Bankes his horse, that rare master of the caballistick art, whose memory is not forgotten in England." The history here alluded to is related in Topsell's History of Four-footed Beasts, 1607, p. 25, and I have seen a copy of that work containing the following manuscript note in a nearly contemporary hand,—"surpassinge Bankes his horse." The notion of his having taught the animal by magical arts has been previously mentioned, and is even introduced by Sir W. Davenant into his burlesque poem on the Long Vacation in London, Works, ed. 1673, p. 291,—

> And white oate-eater that does dwell,
> In stable small at sign of Bell :
> That lift up hoofe to show the prancks,
> *Taught by magitian, stiled Banks ;*
> And ape, led captive still in chaine,
> Till he renounce the Pope and Spaine.
> All these on hoof now trudge from town,
> To cheat poor turnep-eating clown.

A similar imputation seems to be hinted at in Decker's Satiro-Mastix,—" I'll teach thee to turn me into Banks his horse, and to tell gentlemen, I am a jugler, and can show tricks." A character in Randolph's Hey for Honesty, Down with Knavery, 1651, p. 3, speaks of " Banks the conjurer," no doubt intending the same person. In the White Devil, 1612, the horse is alluded to as having been spoken of as a spirit,—"and some there are, will keep a curtal, to shew juggling tricks, and give out 'tis a spirit."

Decker, who very frequently alludes to the exhibition, informs us that the feats were entirely accomplished by signs and words. " There are likewise other barbers who are so well customed that they shave a whole citie sometymes in three dayes, and they doe it, as Bankes his horse did. his tricks, onely by the eye and the eare," Seven Deadly Sinnes of London, 1606. A similar testimony is given by Killigrew, in the Parson's Wedding, 1664,— "she governs them with signs and by the eye, as Banks breeds his horse;" and to these may be added the following general directions by Markham :—" Now you must observe that whilst you teach him thus, looke to what place you point your rod, to that place also you must most constantly place your eie, not remooving it to anie other object til your wil be performed,

for it is your eie and countenance, as wel as
your words, by which the horse is guided; and
whosoever did note Bankes' curtal, might see
that his eie did never part from the eie of his
maister; when your horse wil thus, by the
directions of your rod and your eie, carrie any
thinge you will to the place you shall appoint
him unto, then you shall so hourelie practise
him therein, that in the end if you do make
never so slight a signe with your rod, so your
eie be constantly fixte, yet the horse will beare
it towardes that place, which as oft as hee
doeth, you shal cherish him and give him
food."

A mystery is attached to the fate of Banks
and his horse which has not been satisfactorily
elucidated. They are said to have been burned
at Rome by command of the Pope, a statement
for which the only direct authority, hitherto
discovered, is a marginal note in the mock-
romance of Don Zara del Fogo, 1656, to the
following effect:—" Banks his beast; if it be
lawful to call him a beast, whose perfections
were so incomparably rare, that he was worthily
term'd the four-legg'd wonder of the world for
dancing; some say singing, and discerning
maids from maulkins: finally, having of a long

time proved himself the ornament of the
Brittish clime, travailing to Rome with his
master, they were both burned by the com-
mandment of the Pope." There is a playful
allusion to something of the same kind in Ben
Jonson's Epigrams, Workes, ed. 1616, p. 817,—

> But 'mong'st these Tiberts, who do you thinke there
>     was ?
> Old Bankes the juggler, our Pythagoras,
> Grave tutor to the learned horse.   Both which,
> Being, beyond sea, burned for one witch :
> Their spirits transmigrated to a cat :
> And, now above the poole, a face right fat
> With great gray eyes, are lifted up, and mew'd ;
> Thrise did it spit: thrise div'd.  .  .  .  .
> They cry'd out, Pusse.   He told them he was Bankes,
> That had, so often, shew'd 'hem merry prankes.
> They laugh't at his laugh-worthy fate.   And past
> The tripple head without a sop.

Neither of these testimonies, although they
are not to be disregarded, are absolutely decisive, for they both occur in imaginative pieces
of writing; and they seem to be somewhat
inconsistent with the notices of Banks of a
later date, there being no doubt but that he
is the same personage with a rather celebrated
vintner of the name, who resided in Cheap-

side. That such was the fact is clearly shown by a passage in the Life and Death of Mistress Mary Frith, 1662, p. 75, the author of which says,—"I shall never forget my fellow humourist Banks, the vintner in Cheapside, who taught his horse to dance and shooed him with silver." He appears to have been alive as late as 1637, for in MS. Ashmole 826 is preserved a satirical piece entitled, "A Bill of Fare sent to Bankes the Vintner in Cheapeside, in May, 1637," which is an amusing list of mock-dishes, such as,—"Foure paire of elephants' pettitoes; a greene dragon spring cock; a rhinoceros boyled in alligant; sixe tame lyons in greene sawce; a whole horse sowced after the Russian fashion; the pluck of a grampus stewed: an apes tayle in sippitts; the jole of a whale butterd in barbary viniger," &c. It is, therefore, evident that Ben Jonson's allusion is to an imaginary occurrence, if this date be accepted as genuine. "A parlous head, and yet loving to his guests, as mine host Bankes," Chapman and Shirley's Ball, a Comedy, 1639.

For as true as Bankes his horse knowes a Spaniard from an Englishman, or there went up one and twentie maides to the top of

Boston steeple, and there came but one downe
againe, so true it is that there are men which
have dealt with me in the same humour that
heere I shadowe.—*Nash's Have with You to
Saffron Walden,* 1596.

Another (speech) Bankes pronounced long a-gon,
When he his curtailes qualities exprest . . . .
Yet Bankes his horse is better knowne then he ;
So are the cammels and the westerne hog.
        *Epigrams by J. D. ad fin. Ovid's Elegies,* n. d.

Bankes hath an horse of wondrous qualitie,
For he can fight, and . . . . ., and daunce, and lie,
And finde your purse, and tell what coyne ye have :
But, Bankes, who taught your horse to smel a knave ?
        *Bastard's Chrestoleros,* 12mo. Lond. 1598

*Con.* Sure this baboune is a great Puritane.
—*Bou.* Is not this strange ?—*W. S.* Not a
whit ; by this light, Bankes his horse and hee
were taught both in a stable.—*Ram Alley, or
Merrie Trickes,* 1611.

And certainly, if Banks had lived in elder
times, he would have shamed all the inchanters
of the world, for whosoever was most famous
among them, could never master or instruct
any beast as he did his horse.—*Ralegh's Historie of the World,* ed. 1614, i. 178.

They are at London, George in his chamber at Brainford, accompanied with none but one Anthony Nit, a barber, who dined and supped with him continually, of whom he had borrowed a lute to pass away the melancholy afternoon, of which he could play as well as Banks's horse.—*Peele's Jests*, 1627.

There shall you see an old blind brave baboone,
That can put on the humor of an asse,
Can come aloft, Jack, heigh passe and repasse ;
That for ingenious study downe can put
Old Holden's camell, or fine Bankes his cut.
*A Cast over the Water to W. Fennor ; Taylor's*
*Workes*, ii. 159.

There are some curious allusions to the dancing-horse, as late as 1654, in some verses at the end of Gayton's Pleasant Notes upon Don Quixot, in which it is spoken of as being shooed with silver, as having been to the top of St. Paul's, as dancing to the music of the pipe and being able to count money with its feet. The horse is supposed to be thus addressing the steed of Don Quixote, the verses being entitled,—" Bancks his horse to Rosinant,"—

Though Rosinante famous was in fields
For swiftnesse, yet no horse like me had heels.
Goldsmiths did shoe me, not the Ferri-Fabers ;
One nail of mine was worth their whole weeks labours.

Horse, thou of metall too, but not of gold,—
'Twas best 'twas so, or oft they had been sold,—
Let us compare our feats; thou top of nowles
Of hils hast oft been seen, I top of Paules.
To Smythfield horses I stood there the wonder;
I only was at top; more have been under.
Thou like a Spanish jennet, got i' th' wind,
Wert hoysted by a windmill; 'twas in kinde.
But never yet was seen in Spaine or France,
A horse like Bancks his, that to th' pipe would dance:
Tell mony with his feet; a thing which you,
Good Rosinante nor Quixot e'r could doe.
Yet I doe yield, surpassed in one feat,
Thou art the only horse, that liv'dst sans meat.

A few other notices may be just worth a
reference. "Hee keeps more adoe with this
monster than ever Bankes did with his horse,
or the fellow with the elephant," Every Man
out of his Humor, 1600; "It shall be chroni-
cled next after the death of Bankes' horse,"
Jack Drum's Entertainment, 1601; "Is glad to
shew tricks like Bancks his curtall," Decker's
Wonderfull Yeare, 1603; Armin's Nest of
Ninnies, 1608, repr. p. 40: Stephens' Essayes
and Characters, 1615; "Asses they (the Egyp-
tians) will teach to do such tricks, as if possessed with reason, to whom Banks his horse
would have proved but a zany," Sandys'

Travels, ed. 1615, p. 124; Scot's Philomythie
or Philomythologie, 1616, sig. C; "And more
strange horse-tricks playd by such riders then
Bankes his curtall did ever practise," Decker's
Belmans Night Walkes; Drayton, ii. 186, as
referred to by Nares, in v. *Banks's Horse;*
Aristippus or the Joviall Philosopher, 1630, p.
19; "And Banks his hors shew'd tricks, taught
with much labor," Taylor's Workes, 1630;
"great Banks," Harington's Epigrams, 1633,
iii. 21, the author's MS. reading, *gray Banks;*
"Set him but upon Bankes his horse in a
saddle rampant," Cleaveland's Character of a
London Diurnall, 1647, repeated in the Poems,
ed. 1651, and in the Works, ed. 1687, p. 86;
Cockayn's Obstinate Lady, 1657, p. 32; "It
will good fellows shew more sport, than Bankes
his horse could do," ballad of Little Barley-
corne. It may perhaps be as well to observe
that the term curtail, applied to the horse in
some of these instances, does not necessarily
relate to the mutilation of the tail, which is
shown in its natural proportions in the en-
graving prefixed to Maroccus Extaticus, 1595.

Two other persons of the name of Banks
may perhaps deserve notice, to guard against
the misappropriation of notices not intended

for the subject of this note. Ben Jonson, Workes, ed. 1616, p. 777, has an epigram "on Banck the usurer," other copies of which are in the Witts Recreations, 1654, and in MS. Ashmol. 47. He has also an epigram "on Chuffe, Bancks the Usurer's kinsman," ibid. p. 780. "Banks the broker," mentioned in the Witts Recreations, is perhaps the same person. Master Banks of Waltham is introduced into the Merry Devil of Edmonton, 1608. The name appears to have been a very common one, and a vast number of allusions to individuals bearing it might easily be collected.

# A
# PLEASANT
## Conceited Comedie
### CALLED,
## Loues labors loſt.

As it vvas preſented before her Highnes
this laſt Chriſtmas.

Newly correſted and augmented
By *W. Shakeſpere*.

Imprinted at London by *W.W.*
for *Cutbert Burby.*
1598.

## MEMORANDUM.—1879.

THE preceding observations on Love's Labour's Lost and the Dancing Horse were written by me in the year 1855. The following additional notes are selected from a large parcel which has accumulated since that period.

This comedy was acted before Queen Elizabeth at Whitehall in the Christmas holidays of 1597, the locality of the performance being ascertained from the following interesting entry in the accounts of the Treasurer of the Chamber for that year,—"to Richard Brakenburie, for altering and making readie of soundrie chambers at Whitehall against Christmas, and for the plaies, and for making readie in the hall for her Majestie, and for altering and hanging of the chambers after Christmas daie, by the space of three daies, mense Decembris, 1597, viij.*li.* xiij.*s.* iiij.*d.*"

The term *once*, employed by Tofte, does not mean *formerly*, but merely, as usual in his day, at some time or other. It does nevertheless imply that the representation of the comedy had been witnessed some little time at all events before the publication of his Alba in 1598, but the notice, however curious, is of no value in the question of the chronology, as we are left in doubt whether it was the original or the amended play that was seen by him. The poor fellow had escorted his lady-love to the theatre, and for some unexplained reason she had taken an opportunity during their visit to reject his addresses. The following copy of the verses written on the occasion, which are found in the third part of the Alba, was taken by me many years ago from the extremely rare original edition, then preserved in the Charlemont Library at Dublin,—

Loves Labor Lost, I once did see a Play,
Ycleped so, so called to my paine,
Which I to heare to my small Ioy did stay,
Giuing attendance on my froward Dame,
 My misgiuing minde presaging to me Ill,
 Yet was I drawne to see it gainst my Will.

This *Play* no *Play*, but Plague was vnto me,
For there I lost the Loue I liked most :
And what to others seemde a Iest to be,
I, that (in earnest) found vnto my cost.
 To euery one (saue me) twas *Comicall*,
 Whilst *Tragick* like to me it did befall.

Each Actor plaid in cunning wise his part,
But chiefly Those entrapt in *Cupids* snare :
Yet All was fained, twas not from the hart,
They seemde to grieue, but yet they felt no care :
  Twas I that Griefe (indeed) did beare in brest,
  The others did but make a show in Iest.

Yet neither faining theirs, nor my meere Truth,
Could make her once so much as for to smile :
Whilst she (despite of pitie milde and ruth)
Did sit as skorning of my Woes the while.
  Thus did she sit to see LOVE lose his LOVE,
  Like hardned Rock that force nor power can moue.

Malone considered that "the conceit of *A-jax* and *a-jakes* may not have originated with Harrington, and may hereafter be found in some more ancient tract," Shakespeare's Works, ed. 1821, ii. 329. If so, of course the allusion is not of much value in the chronological enquiry; but Harrington made the quibble so popular that Shakespeare's reference in all probability was written after the appearance of the Metamorphosis in the latter part of 1596, the work having been entered in the Stationers' Registers on October 30th in that year.

With reference to the extract from the Revels' Accounts published by the Shakespeare Society in 1842, it is a most singular circumstance that, although the manuscript Shaksperian entries in the Revels' Book of 1605, now preserved in the Record Office, are unquestionably very modern forgeries, the authentic fact that Love's Labour's Lost was twice performed before James the First early in that year is ascertained from the following note taken from a modernized transcript of the audit accounts made for Malone, who died in the year 1812,—"on New Year's Day and Twelfth Day, Loves Labour Lost performed by the King's players."

Marston, in his Malcontent, 1604, sig. B. 2, makes one of his characters speak of running "the wilde-goose chase even with Pompey the huge," an allusion no doubt to the personage of that name in Love's Labour's Lost.

Francis Smethwick, the son of the publisher of the edition of 1631, entered his ownership of the copyright of Love's Labour's Lost on August 24th, 1642,—"entred for his copies by order of a full Court holden this day all these copies hereafter mencioned, the which did belong unto Mr. John Smethwick his late father deceased, — Hamblett, a play ; the Tameing of a Shrew ; Romeo and Juliett;

Loves Labour Lost." On the 14th of the following month, the entry just cited having no doubt been made in anticipation of the transaction, he assigned his interest to one Flesher,—"assigned over unto him, by vertue of a note under the hand and seale of Francis Smethwick and subscribed by both the wardens, all the estate, right, title and interest which the said Francis hath in these copies hereafter following, the which did lately belong unto Mr. John Smethwick his father deceased,— Hamlett, a play; the Tameing of a Shrew; Romeo and Juliett; Loves Labour Lost."

The following curious anecdote connected with the representation of a rustic speech-play, which may refer to a modernized form of some rude provincial dramatic dialogue that Shakespeare may possibly have heard in his youth, occurs amongst my papers, but I have unfortunately neglected to note whence it was derived,—" In Cumberland it is essential to maskers who are adepts and hope for applause, to perform what is there called a speech play, in contradistinction to mumming or mummery of which the primary import is pantomimical representation. I cannot learn that the speech-plays exhibited on these occasions have ever

been written, much less printed, and I regret
that it has not been in my power to procure
one as spoken. But I happen to remember
a story relating to them which was current in
the county when I was a boy, and which,
though low and ludicrous, is not only a fair
specimen of rustic wit, but also, it may be,
of the theatrical abilities displayed in the
infancy of the drama. One of these maskers,
it is said, as the company could not presume
to aspire to a Chorus, once announced his
character to the audience in these words,
—'I am Hector of Troy;' on which, one
of the people exclaimed,—'Thou, Hector of
Troy! why, thou'rt Jwon Thomson oth'
Lwonin steed — what, didst fancy I'd not
know thee because thou art disguised?' The
play proceeded, and it being necessary to the
conduct of the piece that Hector should die,
this son of the sack, having previously been
instructed that it would not be quite natural
to die instantaneously on his fall, nor without
two or three convulsive pangs, when he fell
on the floor as he had been directed first
fetched a deep groan, counting as it were to
himself the while, was heard to say, *ae pang;*
on fetching another groan he again said,

*twae pangs;* and in like manner, when a third groan was uttered, he said faintly, *three pangs and now I's dead."* John Thompson was anticipated by the recommendation given by Bottom to Snug the Joiner, while the account of the dying scene is curiously analogous to the stage-death of Pyramus by three thrusts of the sword,—" Thus die I,—thus, thus, thus !"

" Loues Labors Lost, comedie," occurs in the list of books read by Drummond of Hawthornden in the year 1606 preserved in manuscript in the library of the Society of Antiquaries of Edinburgh. In MS. Addit. 14,047 in the British Museum is preserved a copy of a play called Love's Hospital dated in 1636. On the fly-leaf of this manuscript is written,—

Loues Hospitall.

Loues Labores Lost.

a circumstance which would appear to show that about that period there was in existence a manuscript transcript of Shakespeare's comedy originally bound up with the other play. Let us hope that this may some day turn up.

There is a fine and perfect copy, very clean and genuine, of the first edition of Love's Labour's Lost in the Drummond collection preserved in the University Library at Edinburgh. There is, however, a minute hole in sig. A. 3, and a few of the head-lines are slightly cut into. Drummond has altered the word *affection* in act v. sc. 1 to *affectation*, the modernized form afterwards adopted in the edition of 1632.

In act iv. sc. 3 there is a well-known speech in which, in the original copies, parts of the author's first sketch are mixed up with the text of the corrected drama. It is the one by Biron commencing,—*'Tis more than need.* This speech has continued in an unsatisfactory state from the appearance of the first edition in 1598 to the present day. The arrangement given by Capell, adopted by Dyce, appears to be the best yet suggested ; but objections may be taken to it. Is it certain that the four lines commencing, " Learning is but an adjunct," formed a rejected part of the original play ? The fact appears to be that what is preserved of the latter commences with these five lines,—

> For when would you, my Lord, or you, or you,
> Have found the ground of study's excellence
> Without the beauty of a woman's face ?
> For where is any author in the world
> Teaches such beauty as a woman's eye ?

for although the two last lines may at first seem to form a connected part of the later composition, a little consideration will show that they are out of place and injuriously anticipate the argument that follows. In the place of the above lines Shakespeare wrote as follows,—

> For when would you, my liege, or you, or you,
> In leaden contemplation have found out
> Such fiery numbers as the prompting eyes
> Of beauty's tutors have enrich'd you with ?

The next piece of the original play seems to be contained in the following lines,—

> From women's eyes this doctrine I derive ;
> They are the ground, the books, the academes
> From whence doth spring the true Promethean fire.

thus altered by Shakespeare,—

> From women's eyes this doctrine I derive ;
> They sparkle still the right Promethean fire ;
> They are the books, the arts, the academes,
> That show, contain and nourish all the world ;
> Else none at all in ought proves excellent.

and, finally, there can be no doubt that the following two lines,—

> O, we have made a vow to study, lords,
> And in that vow we have forsworn our books.

are the original drafts of,—

> And where that you have vow'd to study, lords,
> In that each of you have forsworn his book,
> Can you still dream and pore and thereon look ?

These variations are of extreme interest as exhibiting the careful revision of the first text, that text having undoubtedly been one of Shakespeare's earliest complete dramatic productions. It is very unlikely that the revision was made immediately after the appearance of the original play, and the internal evidence does not appear to render the date of 1597 for the amended copy an impossibility. We must bear in mind that the enlarged comedy would most likely retain the general construction and specialities of the original, so that here at least the tests of metre and style are of no avail. And, indeed, the latter are seldom of decisive use excepting when they are made entirely subservient to arguments founded on the more positive criteria of dramatic power and characterization.

In William Shakspere a Biography, by Charles Knight, there is an attempt to show that the pageant of the Nine Worthies was a parody on an ancient one first exhibited at

Coventry at the reception of Henry the Sixth
in the year 1455, and that Shakespeare had
seen a representation of the latter. There is
not the slightest evidence or probability that
this old pageant, written for a special occasion,
was ever performed at a later period. Amongst
the Loseley manuscripts of the time of Edward
the Sixth is a list of " properties and weapons
provided for a mask of Greek Worthyes."
These Worthies were frequent subjects of
dramatic representation. " Divers play Alex-
ander on the stages," observes Williams in
his Discourse of Warre, 1590, " but fewe or
none in the field."

The exquisitely descriptive song-dialogue
between Spring and Winter may possibly have
been suggested,—I mean the idea of such a
dialogue—by a very old black-letter poem
entitled, " The Debate and Stryfe betwene
Somer and Wynter," imprynted by me laurens
andrew to sell at the signe of seynt Johan
Evangelyst in saynt Martyns parysshe besyde
Charynge Crosse. The notion long continued
to be somewhat of a favourite one. At the
close of the Christmas Ordinary, a privately
acted comedy printed in 1682, is a brief " show
of the four parts of the year contending for

priority," in which Ver, Summer, Autumn and Hyems, argue in separate speeches.

With respect to the title of Shakespeare's play it is worthy of remark that, in the list of the comedies prefixed to the first folio it is given as "Loues Labour lost." The same form is also seen in the list of plays appended to the comedy of Tom Tyler, 1661, and in Kirkman's list, 4to. 1671. I have a memorandum that the name of the comedy was perhaps suggested by lines in the Handful of Pleasant Delights, 1584, "ye loving wormes," &c., sig. C. 6, but I have no convenient means just now of referring to that work.

These memoranda on Love's Labour's Lost may be appropriately concluded with the following additional collections on the Dancing Horse, the certainty of Shakespeare's allusion being confirmed by the extract from Old Meg of Herefordshire, 1609, given at p. 44.

Banks was a native of Staffordshire, and it would seem that he must have taught more than one horse to perform the marvellous tricks, the first being a white and the other a bay one. This appears from the following very interesting account preserved in a contemporary manuscript diary kept by a native of Shrewsbury,—"September, 1591, 33 Eliz. This yeare and against the assise tyme on Master Banckes, a Staffordshire gentile, brought into this towne of Salop a white horsse whiche wolld doe woonderfull and strange thinges, as thesse,—wold in a company or prese tell howe many peeces of money by hys foote were in a mans purce ; also, yf the partie his master wolld name any man beinge hyd never so secret in the company, wold fatche hym owt with his mowthe, either naming hym the veriest knave in the company, or what cullerid coate he hadd ; he pronowncid further to his horse and said, Sirha, there be two baylyves in the towne, the one of them bid mee welcom unto this towne and usid me in frindly maner ; I wold have the goe to hym and gyve hym thanckes for mee ; and he wold goe truly to the right baylyf that did so use hys sayd master as he did in the sight of a number of people, unto Master Baylyffe Sherar, and bowyd unto hym in makinge curchey withe hys foote in sutche maner as he coullde, withe suche strange feates for sutche a beast to doe, that many people judgid that it were impossible to be don except he had a famyliar or don by the arte of magicke."

"O, how much art thou beholding to thy legs! Bankes was not so much beholding to his horse that served to ride on and to doo such wonderfull crankes, as thou art to thy leggs which have thus cunningly conveyed thee," The Trimming of Thomas Nashe, 1597.

*Of Bankes and his horse.*—Bankes being at Orleance in France and making his famous horse do tricks, which to the French seemed so strange and wonderfull that they thought they could not be done without the helpe of the divell, the monkes and friars caused him to be apprehended and brought him before the magistrate, and accused him to be a witch or a conjurer; whereupon Banks desired them he might send for his horse and then he would give them a plaine demonstration that hee was no divell. They granted his request, and when the horse was come, hee entreated one of them to hold up his crucifixe before the horse, which hee no sooner did but the horse kneeled downe before it, whereat they greatly marvelled, and saying the beast was inspired, dismissed Banks not without money and great commendations.— *The Booke of Bulls*, 1636.

Mr. Elliot Browne, in Notes and Queries of 11 Nov. 1876, gives an interesting notice of

Banks and his horse from a French work of 1626. Mr. William Chappell mentions Banks's Game, a tune which was played while Banks was exhibiting his horse. "His eye observes Master Attourney, as Banks' horse did his master," Hogs Character of a Projector, 1642. "Not much of an higher pitch then what hath been related of an horse that by the help of a hot floore and some traces was taught to dance · to a tune," Hammond of a Late or a Death-bed Repentance, 1646. "Bancks of London who taught his horse reason to perform feats above belief," Fuller's Worthies, 1662. "She governes them with signes and by the eye, as Banks breedes his horse," Parson's Wedding, a comedy, 1663. "I think verily that neither Doctor Faustus nor Banks his horse could ever do such admirable feats, although it is sure they had a devil to help them," Mun's Englands Treasure by Forraign Trade, 1664, p. 116.

# KING JOHN.

Some of the prominent incidents of the reign of King John were selected by Bishop Bale, about the middle of the sixteenth century, certainly before the year 1563, the date of the bishop's decease, for the subject of a play, entitled Kynge Johan, in which that sovereign's disputes with the Pope are made the vehicles of an application to the circumstances of the Reformation and to the state of England during the latter part of the reign of Henry the Eighth, especially with reference to the struggles of the people with the Church of Rome. This drama, which is the earliest known example of an English play constructed with reference to events of history, was never printed, but the original manuscript, partly in the author's handwriting, and throughout carefully corrected by him, is in the possession of the Duke of Devonshire, and has been published under the editorship of Mr. J. P.

Collier, 4to. 1838. The historical characters in this production are King John, Pope Innocent, Cardinal Pandulph, Archbishop Langton, the monk Simon of Swineshead and another called Raymondus. There are also several abstract impersonations, namely, England, represented as a widow ; Imperial Majesty, who is supposed to take the reins of government after King John has been poisoned ; the three estates of Nobility, Clergy, and Civil Order, representing the magistracy ; Treason, Verity, and Sedition, the last of whom is the Vice or jester. The introduction of the latter allegorical impersonations imparts to the work the character of a morality, but in all essential respects it may be considered a genuine historical play. King John is here represented as a chivalrous and generous sovereign whose exertions to benefit his country are neutralised by the malice of the clergy, instead of the ruler whose want of principle involves him in all the horrors of gloomy and timorous guilt, as he is depicted by Shakespeare. Bale's play is in two parts, the colophon being as follows,—" Thus endeth the ij. playes of Kynge Johan," but, owing to some defect in the manuscript, the exact division intended by the author is not clearly ascertained, though it is obviously too long for a single performance, and there can be no doubt but that it is an early example of a practice, afterwards common, of the separation of a drama into parts for the convenience of representation. No information is accessible with respect to the period or locality in which it was performed, but it is unlikely to have been for any length of time a popular composition, and, as it was never published in the sixteenth century, it is in the highest degree improbable that any part of it was known to the author or authors of a subsequent drama on the events of the same historical era, also in two parts, which was published in 1591 under the title of, " The Troublesome Raigne of Iohn King of England, with the discouerie of King Richard Cordelions base sonne (vulgarly named the Bastard Fawconbridge) : also the death of King Iohn at Swinstead Abbey. As it was (sundry times) publikely acted by the Queenes Maiesties Players, in the honourable Citie of London. Imprinted at London for Sampson Clarke, and are to be solde at his shop, on the backe side of the Royall Exchange, 1591." A separate title to

the second part of this edition is as follows,—
" The second part of the troublesome Raigne
of King Iohn, conteining the death of Arthur
Plantaginet, the landing of Lewes, and the
poysning of King Iohn at Swinstead Abbey.
As it was (sundry times) publikely acted by
the Queenes Maiesties Players, in the honourable Citie of London. Imprinted at London
for Sampson Clarke, and are to be solde at his
shop, on the backe-side of the Royall Exchange. 1591." This production is of great
interest, Shakespeare, following the custom
adopted by his professional contemporaries,
having constructed an abridged drama out of
the materials afforded by this inferior old play,
but making, as usual, the subject so entirely
his own as to preclude the suggestion of
plagiarism in the objectionable sense of that
term. The name of the author of the Troublesome Raigne of John is not known, the attri-
bution of it to Rowley and others not being
supported by any evidence. Pope asserts
(ed. 1723, p. 148) as if speaking from tradi-
tional knowledge, that it was the joint production of Shakespeare and William Rowley, but
if any writer of the latter name were concerned
in the authorship, it could hardly be Rowley

the actor, but rather the Maister Rowley, whom Meres alludes to in 1598 as "once a rare scholar of learned Pembroke Hall in Cambridge." The former Rowley married as late as 1637, and was a player in the King's Company in 1625, his first work appearing in 1607. In the first edition of 1591, are the following lines, addressed "to the gentlemen readers,"—

> You that with friendly grace of smoothed brow
> Have entertaind the Scythian Tamburlaine,
> And given applause unto an infidel;
> Vouchsafe to welcome, with like curtesie,
> A warlike Christian and your countreyman.
> For Christ's true faith indur'd he many a storme,
> And set himselfe against the man of Rome,
> Until base treason by a damned wight,
> Did all his former triumphs put to flight.
> Accept of it, sweete gentles, in good sort,
> And thinke it was prepard for your disport.

which have been supposed to indicate that Marlowe was the author of the work, but it certainly proves no more than that Tamburlaine the Great, published in the preceding year, 1590, met with the success here solicited on behalf of the old King John. The lines were probably only inserted at the suggestion of the bookseller, and are not to be accepted as a prologue attached to the original manuscript of the play. Some trifling similarities of thought and diction to be traced in this tragedy, and others to which Marlowe is believed to have largely contributed, are too insignificant to warrant the deduction of any theory of authorship beyond the enunciation of a possibility that Marlowe may have been concerned with others in the composition of the Troublesome Raigne ; but, on the whole, considering its style, the probability is that the entire work is the production of one or more authors whose names are yet to be discovered. It was republished in the year 1611, under the following title,—"The first and second Part of the troublesome Raigne of John King of England. With the discouerie of King Richard Cordelions Base sonne (vulgarly named, the Bastard Fawconbridge :) Also, the death of King Iohn at Swinstead Abbey. As they were (sundry times) lately acted by the Queenes Maiesties Players. Written by W. Sh. Imprinted at London by Valentine Simmes for Iohn Helme, and are to be sold at his shop in Saint Dunstons Churchyard in Fleetestreet. 1611." The publisher of this edition, it will be observed, inserted the deceptive letters W. Sh. as indicative of the author, and carefully altered the statement that the play had been " publicly acted in the City of London," the company to which Shakespeare belonged having no public theatre within the precincts of the City, their only City theatre being the Blackfriars', a private playhouse. The lines addressed to the reader, cited above, were omitted. The expression, " lately acted," may have been inserted with the view to lead the intending purchaser to the belief that it was Shakespeare's play, the older drama having been then probably superseded; but the retention of the word *Queenes* may perhaps show that this edition of 1611 was a mere reprint in every particular of an unknown impression which may have appeared between the year 1591 and the death of Queen Elizabeth. It may be worthy of remark that the printer of it appears to have had a deficient supply of type of the letter *e*, which is misprinted *c* no fewer than sixty times in the course of the play ; at least, such is the case in the copy in my possession. In the next edition, issued in 1622, the name of Shakespeare was boldly given at full length,

—" The first and second Part of the troublesome Raigne of Iohn King of England. With
the discouerie of King Richard Cordelions
base sonne (vulgarly named, the Bastard
Fauconbridge :) Also the death of King Iohn
at Swinstead Abbey. As they were (sundry
times) lately acted. Written by W. Shakespeare. London, Printed by Aug : Mathewes
for Thomas Dewe, and are to be sold at
his shop in St. Dunstones Churchyard in
Fleet-street, 1622." In this edition, notwith-
standing that the first title includes both parts,
there is a second one in which the name of
Shakespeare is also conspicuously given,—
" The Second Part of the Troublesome Raigne
of King John, containing the entrance of
Lewis, the French Kings sonne, with the
poysoning of King John by a Monke. Written
by W. Shakespeare. London, Printed by
Aug : Mathewes for Thomas Dewe, and are
to be sold at his shop in St. Dunstones
Churchyard in Fleet-street, 1622." There
had been no doubt a demand for Shakespeare's play, but that not being accessible,
and retained by the stage-managers, the older
drama was reprinted under the shelter of his
popular name. Langbaine, writing in 1691,

speaking of the two parts of the latter play,
observes,—" these plays are not divided into
acts, neither are the same with that in folio.
I am apt to conjecture that these were first
writ by our author, and afterwards revised and
reduced into one play by him : that in the folio
being far the better;" a conjecture that has
been revived of late years, but it is improbable,
judging only from internal evidence, and no
other testimony of value is accessible, that our
great poet had much share in the composition
of the older play, a work of great merit for the
age at which it appeared, but written in a style
bearing small trace of the hand of Shakespeare
beyond the occasional fondness of the writer
for jingling repetitions of words, a peculiarity
not in itself sufficiently marked to be considered a test of authorship, and a few pathetic
touches of expression that are scarcely un-
worthy of his pen, to which may be added, as
the possible rough draft and an author's early
attempt, the spirited delineation of the character of Falconbridge so inimitably elaborated
into an almost new personage by Shakespeare.
The main story and dramatic arrangement of
the old play are faithfully copied by our great
dramatist, who has also adopted a few of the

lines (slightly altered) as well as two complete
lines and some expressions, but his amplifica-
tions of scenes and speeches are strikingly
original and the variations and omissions of
incidents are made with consummate judge-
ment. It is worthy of remark that Shakespeare does not adopt in any shape those
portions of the Troublesome Raigne which
satirize the depravity of the monastic orders,
but that he confines his denunciation of the
papistical system to the tyrannical and usurping
tendency exhibited by the court of Rome.
The dramatis personæ are nearly the same in
both plays, the only character added by Shakespeare being James Gurney, servant to Lady
Falconbridge. He has, however, omitted a
few personages who are introduced by his
predecessor, such as the Earls of Chester and
Clare, Lord Beauchamp, the Abbot of Swinstead, &c.

The exact period at which Shakespeare
adapted the incidents of the preceding drama
to his own purposes in the composition of his
history of King John is unknown, but the
latter must have appeared before 1598, as
it is mentioned in the list of his tragedies in
the Palladis Tamia of Meres, published in that

year, where it is classed with Richard the
Second, Richard the Third, Henry the Fourth,
and others. It was probably written after
1591, the date of the publication of the
Troublesome Raigne, but still it is possible
that Shakespeare may have used a play-house
copy of that piece, so that a limit in that
direction can hardly be determined with certainty. There are no allusions in the play
itself that can be safely depended upon as
arguments in the question respecting the date
of its composition, with the exception, perhaps,
of the reference, in the first act, to a passage in
the tragedy of Solyman and Perseda, which
was entered on the books of the Stationers'
Company in November, 1592, and was probably then in the commencement of its popularity. Various passages have been supposed
to allude to events of the author's time, but in
no instance is there any evidence of Shakespeare having intended to apply the circumstances of this drama to those of his own era,
and, in the absence of proof, it is most reason-
able to conclude that he had no design of the
kind. King John was not printed until 1623,
when it appeared with the other histories in
the first folio edition, and it is worthy of

remark that it is the only authentic play of Shakespeare that is not named in any way in the Registers of the Stationers' Company. It is not even mentioned in the long list of his plays, amongst "soe manie of the said copies as are not formerly entred to other men," which is inserted in the registers, under the date of November, 1623, the long entry made by Blount and Jaggard preparatory to the issue of the collective edition of the poet's works. Unless, as was probably the case, the omission was accidental, there may either have been a previous entry of the play to some other publisher, although such entry is not now to be found in the register, or the copyright of King John belonged to one of the publishers whose general rights had been purchased by Blount and Jaggard. The play, in the folio editions, is entitled, "the Life and Death of King John," the term "life" probably referring to his life as a sovereign, as there is no portion of the tragedy which refers to his history previously to his accession to the throne of England, which took place in May, 1199.

The plot of this drama being chiefly founded on that of an earlier play, with merely a few incidents suggested by a recollection of other sources, either the chronicles of Holinshed and others, or old historical ballads, it is obvious that any attempt to reconcile the narrative with the exact facts of history would be irrelevant. The tragedy is undoubtedly invested with additional interest from the circumstance of its characters belonging to a momentous period of English history, and some of its incidents being romantic pictures of real events, but it is to be judged, in its character as a work of art, essentially as if the whole were imaginary, it being, in fact, a production the merits of which do not depend on its connexion with a particular era of the world's annals. Shakespeare and other writers of this department have merely made use of historical materials for dramatic purposes, without any necessary reference to the exactitude of history; so that an endeavour to exhibit the poet in the light of an historian, to correct with minuteness his numerous errors in dates, events, and even confusions of personages, or to reconcile the inconsistencies arising from his defiant neglect of chronology, is not required. Shakespeare, in delineating some of the chief personages introduced into his historical plays, has, with marvellous genius, elaborated the salient points of their characters as known to the public through the chronicles, ballads, poems, dramas and other works of the sixteenth century; but there can be little doubt that any coincidences, not thus to be traced, between the results of diligent historical enquiry and the views taken of secret political workings and traits of eminent men are accidental; or, at most, are to be referred merely to the power of the author's genius in estimating the characters of men from the obscure indications of them given in the sources above alluded to. There is little of this, however, to be traced in the tragedy of King John, which partakes more than any of the other histories of the character of the romantic drama, both in the want of attention paid to the truth and the succession of historical events, and in the manner in which they are made subservient to the purposes of dramatic design.

## MEMORANDA.—1879.

The preceding observations on King John were written by me in the year 1859, and in the long interval that has since elapsed nothing of the slightest importance respecting that play has fallen under my notice.

Hayward, in his Annals of Queen Elizabeth, written in the year 1612, thus imitates a passage in King John,—"Excellent Queene! what doe my words but wrong thy worth? what doe I but guild gold? what but shew the sunne with a candle in attempting to prayse thee."

Heywood, in the Second Part of Edward the Fourth, first printed in 1600, appears to have had the play of King John in his recollection when he wrote,—

> —— Be thy voice
> As fierce as thunder, to affright his soul.
> Herald, be gone, I say! and be thy breath
> Piercing as lightning, and thy words as death!

The story of the death of King John by poison is adopted both in Bale's Kynge Johan and the old play, the authors of which appear to have used the same source of information ; and it is also the subject of an ancient ballad by Deloney, printed in 1607, entitled, The Lamentable Death of King John, how he was poysoned in the Abby at Swinsted by a Fryer. Another story is that the monk Simon placed before the King a dish of pears, most of which he had pricked with a poisoned needle. The latter tale is alluded to in Browne's Britannia's Pastorals, ii. 3. The incident of the drinking wassail, found in both the plays above mentioned, is also to be seen in Grafton's Chronicle, 1569. It may be worth naming that the story of the poisoning rests upon very slender foundations, being mentioned by no contemporary historian, the earliest chronicler who alludes to it being Bartholomew de Cotton, a monk of Norwich, who flourished about the year 1298.

## OTHELLO.

THE twelfth Public Act which was passed in the first Parliament of James the First, some time between March 19th and July 7th, 1604, was levelled "against conjuration, witchcrafte and dealinge with evill and wicked spirits." In the course of this Act it is enacted that, " if any person or persons shall, from and after the feaste of Saint Michaell the Archangell next comminge, take upon him or them, *by witchcrafte, inchantment, charme or sorcerie,* to tell or declare in what place any treasure of golde or silver should or might be founde or had in the earth or other secret places, or where goodes or thinges loste or stollen should be founde or be come, *or to the intent to provoke any person to unlawfull love,*" then such person or persons, if convicted, " shall for the said offence suffer imprisonment by the space of one whole yere without baile or maineprise, and once in everie quarter of the saide yere shall, in some markett towne upon the markett day, or at such tyme as any faire shal be kept there, stand openlie uppon the pillorie by the space of sixe houres, and there shall openlie confesse his or her error and offence." It seems probable that part of the first Act of Othello would not have assumed the form it does, had not the author been familiar with the Statute, in common with the public of the day, the Duke referring to such a law when he tells Brabantio that his accusation of the employment of witch-craft shall be impartially investigated. If this be the case, the date of the composition of this tragedy may be positively assigned to 1604, in which year it was certainly in existence, even allowing that the Audit Office MS. is a forgery.

Since writing the above, it has occurred to me that the offence named in the Statute refers not to the use of charms to make people love one another, but to the employment of them for the provocation of "unlawful love," yet still this may be said to have an oblique application to the story of the tragedy in the surreptitious marriage of Othello. By the Act of James a previous one, 5 Eliz. c. 16, of a similar character was "utterlie" repealed, and the object of the second Act appears to have been to punish the same offence more severely.

In some places in the first folio the name of Othello's perfect wife is given as Desdemon, corresponding to the Greek for *unfortunate.* See Upton, ed. 1746, p. 288. Some stage-loving parent, who no doubt had been taken with the performance of the tragedy at the Globe, gave the name to one of his daughters in 1609, in which year "Catherine and Dezdi-monye, the daughters of William Bishoppe, were baptised the xiiij.th of September" at St. Leonard's, Shoreditch.

The name of Iago occurs in the ancient history of Wales. See the Historie of Cam-bria, 1584, p. 59. "Iago, cousin of Gurgustius, raigned 25 yeeres; for his evill government he died of a litargie and was buried at Yorke," Stowe, A.D. 636.

## ROMEO AND JULIET.

IT is very singular, but the tendency of my researches is to prove that Shakespeare never invented a name. I am every now and then coming upon contemporary evidence to that effect. When Peter says to the First Musician, —"why, music with her silver sound? What say you, Simon Catling?," the apparently obvious conclusion would be that the musician's name was an imaginary one taken from that of the small lute-string so called. A few years ago, to my utter astonishment, I came upon an Elizabethan manuscript which noticed a Symon Catlyn, who was contemporary with Shakespeare, and resided in Southwark not very far from the theatres, a veritable individual in all probability well known to the poet.

The delightful episode of the Apothecary was mainly suggested by some lines in the old poem, but it seems very probable that Shakespeare had also in his recollection the account of Thebane in the Philocopo of Boccaccio, an English translation of which appeared in 1567,

—"having travailed a long while, he sodainly espied before him at the foote of a mountaine a man not yong, nor of to many yeres, small and very spare of person, whose attire shewed him to be but poore, who romed hither and thither gathering herbs, and with a little knife digged up sundry rootes whereof he had filled one of the skirts of his cote ; whom, as Tarolfo saw, he saluted him, and after asked him who he was, of whence and what he made there at so timely an houre. To whome the old man answered,—I am of Thebes and Thebane is my name, and I go up and downe this plaine gathering of these herbes to the end that with the juyce thereof I make divers necessarie and profitable things for divers infirmities whereby I may have wherewithall to live ; and to come at this houre, *it is neede and not delight that constraineth me.*"

The notion that the allusion to this play, in Weever's Epigrammes, is any evidence of its existence before the publication of that work in 1599, will not bear the test of examination.

J. O. H.-P.

Hollingbury Copse,
Brighton.
*December,* 1879.

PRINTED BY J. E. ADLARD, BARTHOLOMEW CLOSE.